Scattered Flowers

The Tara Chadwick Series
Scattered Flowers

Jerry B. Jenkins

MOODY PRESS
CHICAGO

JERRY B. JENKINS

ISBN: 0-8024-8545-6

3 4 5 6 Printing/LC/Year 94 93 92 91

Printed in the United States of America

To Matt Jugunic

Contents

1

Winning and Losing

Tara missed Suzanne. It wasn't that the former best friends never saw each other. They had seen each other every day till the end of the school year, at every practice of the Panda softball team, and, of course, at every game.

But Suzanne had not spoken to Tara for months. Oh, there were those occasional times when she had to be pleasant —when parents or other adults were around and Tara forced the conversation. Suzanne responded, usually without enthusiasm and never looking directly at Tara.

The loss of Suzanne's friendship nearly broke Tara's heart. She was at a point in her life when she needed a close friend in a bad way. There were those she could talk to, but none were her age. Few really understood the joy of being an all-star fast-pitch softball pitcher, of seeing her team win each of its last ten games to clinch the league title. Who could she talk to about being featured in the paper as the perfect pitcher, the girl who had thrown the only perfect game (not allowing even one base runner, not even on a walk or an error) in league history?

Tara wasn't one to brag, but she sure wished she could share the fun of being named the Most Valuable Player in the league and of winning the batting championship—and even the home run title. The Pandas were on their way to the city championship tournament for the first time ever, and even though Suzanne was an important member of the team and knew what it all meant, Tara couldn't enjoy it with her.

When Tara came off the mound after winning the last game of the regular season and clinching the title with one of her three no-hitters (she finished the regular season with ten wins and two losses), she was surrounded by cheering team-mates—except for Suzanne.

Tara fought hard not to think she was somebody special. She knew she was a great player for a girl her age; she would have had to be stupid to not realize that.

She had worked hard and tried to apply the same mind to her game as she had applied to making the honor roll at school, but she also knew that much of her athletic ability was a gift. And since she had begun a new, personal friendship with God during spring break, she knew where that gift came from too.

Yet it was that same new experience, that friendship with God—that knowledge that Jesus Christ cared about her and loved her and had made it possible for her to know God—that cost her her best friend.

Tara spun off the mound and into the arms of her team-mates. They slapped her hands, hugged her, patted her on the back, mashed her hat down into her short, blond hair, and smiled at her. They comically tried to lift her off the ground and carry her on their shoulders, but they all wound up tumbling onto the infield grass.

When they jumped up, she continued to accept congratu-latory handshakes, reaching out to each one in turn, receiving their hand slaps and returning them. A Panda uniform ap-peared in the corner of her eye, and she thrust out her hand, palm up. Her heart sank as Suzanne merely looked at it and her and kept moving.

How could it be? How could a friendship that had gone through so much, lasted so many years, seen so many laughs and so many tears, be torn apart by a simple decision, a simple prayer?

Tara had come to believe that she needed God. After hearing about Him all her life, wondering about Him, trying to pray to Him, thinking about what He meant to her and her family, she had finally learned, finally understood. While at her cousin's house over spring break, during the lowest point in her life, she had seen what it could mean to really know God. She had got a glimpse from her aunt and her uncle and her cousins how wonderful it was to know God personally.

Tara had admitted to Him that she needed Him, that she knew the wrong things she had done in her life had separated her from Him, that she knew Jesus Christ—because He had died for her and her sin—was the only One who could make it possible for her to come to God. And so she did.

Not only had becoming a Christian not solved all Tara's problems, but it had seemed to make them worse. The reason she had been sent to her aunt and uncle's over spring break in the first place was that her parents had split up. Her father had fallen in love with his young secretary. Tara's mother had found out. At first he promised to give up the new woman, Sally Graves, but Mrs. Chadwick soon discovered he had not given her up.

She made Tara's father leave, and now she wanted a divorce. Tara's mother was angry and hurt, and she wanted revenge. Mr. Chadwick was not to see or try to talk to his children.

Tara had been terribly frustrated, believing with all her heart that, if she could talk to her father, she could make him see how terrible a mistake he had made. She was convinced that once he saw her tears, he would come running back to her mother to put everything back the way it had been before.

At first she had not believed any of the stories about him and his new girl friend. She couldn't believe he had his own apartment and had lived with the woman for months. But even when she learned it was all true, she would not be convinced that the situation was hopeless. She wanted to see him, wanted to talk to him, tried to persuade her mother to take him back.

That, she knew, was why her mother thought it best for her to fly several hundred miles away from home this spring. Tara hated the idea, fought to stay home, planned to be miserable. But her Aunt Bev O'Neil and her Uncle Dale were wonderful people. Her cousin Dallas was also an athlete. He was not as good a student as she was, but their interests were similar.

The O'Neils were not wealthy like the Chadwicks, but there was something simple and loving and warm and wonderful about their family. Dallas actually got along with his little sisters most of the time. His best friend, Jimmy Calabresi, was fun and funny, and it was at the Calabresi place that Tara had looked into the sky and wondered about the God who had created such beauty.

She had gone to church all her life, but God had been distant, a Being to be studied and revered and gazed at in stained glass windows and classic paintings. Here was a girl who felt guilty, frustrated, responsible for her parents' breakup. She didn't know why. She just believed that she had done or said something or not done or not said something that caused her parents to not love each other anymore.

Her father couldn't or wouldn't talk to her. Her mother was distracted, short-tempered, almost mean, because of the pressure and the pain. What Tara felt, she came to realize, was that she was alone, that no one cared for or loved her as they once had. Her family, her world, was falling apart, and nothing remained as it once was.

The O'Neils and Jimmy saw God as a friend, Jesus as a Savior, and it was all so natural, even logical. Tara's mother had warned Tara that her aunt, Mrs. Chadwick's younger sister, was "religious, zealous, unbalanced," and that she might try to "force God" on her.

But Tara had found the opposite. The O'Neils hadn't made a big issue out of religion or church or even God. They just included Him in conversations and in life as the all-important Person He was. And they answered her questions. Nothing was forced, pushed, pressured. It had been her decision alone to come to God, to receive Christ.

Her mother was none too thrilled by it, but at least she had come to believe that Tara had made the decision on her own. Though Tara had seen her father upon her return to Milwaukee, she let him do all the talking and didn't even tell him what had happened to her. She did learn, however, that everything she had heard about her father was true, even that he would try to convince her that his new love was wonderful. He had wanted her to meet and get to know and like Sally Graves. Tara had refused.

Later she had gone to see Sally on her own in a caper Suzanne had called Operation Cemetery (because of Sally's last name), when the two best friends had still been speaking. Tara's conversation with Sally had turned everything upside down.

It was amazing to everybody involved that Tara could still concentrate on her schoolwork and her softball with everything that had happened since she talked to Sally. She had finished the school year on the high honor roll and had won the league championship for the Pandas. The next step was the city championship tournament as one of the eight league winners. After that was the state tournament, but no one was even dreaming that far ahead yet.

Coming off the field had become the most embarrassing, awkward moment in Tara's life. Her family had taken a renewed interest in her game, now that she had had so much success. So her mother was there—school was out and she didn't have to stay home to put Tara's little brother, Ray, to bed. Her big brother, Jeff, was there with his girl friend.

Jeff was sad and angry because he had been kicked off the school track team for drinking and smoking. Though he said he had never tried drugs, he ran around with guys who were known druggies, and that got him in trouble too. His girl friend came to the games with him, but it was clear she didn't know what to think about him anymore, and Tara guessed they wouldn't be going together too much longer.

Her father was there too, sitting far away from her mother. Oddly, Sally Graves had also begun showing up at Tara's games, but she sat just as far from Tara's father as he sat from her mother. Mr. Chadwick was a man who had lost both the women in his life. He was miserable and sick.

Sally didn't come to cause trouble. In fact, she tried to blend into the crowd and not make it obvious that she was there. She came only to see Tara, not to make life difficult for her family. But when Tara came off the field, who was she supposed to go to?

She loved Jeff but didn't trust him. She felt bad for him, but she had warned him. She loved Ray, but he was too young to understand what had happened to her, and she had been forbidden to talk to him about her faith.

She loved her mother, and her mother was grateful for whatever it was Tara had said to Sally Graves that had made her leave her father's apartment and tell him she didn't want to live with him or even see him anymore.

Tara loved her father, yet she heard that he blamed her for both his loss of Sally and for the refusal of his wife to take him back. It was a miserable, messy situation, and Tara's only escape was her softball. When she was on that mound, setting, winding, firing pitch after pitch, she could get away from all her troubles.

She was free. When she caught a glimpse of someone from her family, thoughts of disappointment and guilt flooded her mind, but she forced them away. She prayed she could concentrate on the game. She pretended the other team's hitters were the reasons her life was not the same as it had been.

She was grateful that in a strange way her troubles had brought her to God, but her troubles were still there. There was so little she could do about them that she enjoyed pretending that by striking out her opponents she was somehow punishing someone for messing up her life.

It made her an incredible pitcher. And now that the game was over, the league title was won by the Pandas for the first time, and five hundred people were cheering, she slowly moved off the diamond toward the dugout.

She knew that Sally would be quickly heading for her car. Jeff would be in a serious, frustrating conversation with his girl friend, trying to convince her that he had changed and would once again be worthy of her. Her mother would be smiling, accepting congratulations for Tara from people who knew her, all the while trying to herd Ray toward the car so she could once again ignore and elude her husband.

Tara's father would stand at the edge of the crowd, his attention no longer on Tara but now on her mother. He would stand there looking hopeful and sheepish, pleading with his eyes for the chance to just talk to her for a moment, to tell her how sorry he was, to tell her how lonely it was to live in the apartment he had rented for his new girl friend, who had now left him.

2

Chaos

Panda Coach Danielle Andrews was Tara's oasis during those days. Having discovered that her coach was also a Christian, Tara got permission from her mother to spend more time with Danielle. So now, as the team left the field, Tara looked for that smile from her coach that would tell her she had a friend, someone who believed in her, was behind her, win or lose.

It hurt Tara that her family began coming to every game only when the Pandas had emerged as one of the best teams in the city. They had not come just for her, then, but rather to share in the excitement, the glory. Danielle, on the other hand, would have been there anyway, just for Tara.

Tara chuckled as she thought that Danielle would have been there with or without Tara because that was her job. But now as a friend, Tara knew the type of person Danielle was. Danielle had prayed with her, read the Bible with her, counseled Tara in her new faith.

They had had to be careful not to be too obvious about their friendship so it wouldn't make any of the other players jealous. Tonight there would be a party at Danielle's parents' home, and it wouldn't be so apparent that Tara would be the last to leave. That would give her and Danielle time to talk.

At the party there was so much Tara wanted to talk to Danielle about. Like the fact that Suzanne was at the party only for a brief time and that she left with a couple of other girls who had also begun to act cool toward Tara. Could they be jealous? Tara tried hard not to act like she thought she was something special. What more could she do?

After pizza and lots of fun, the girls' parents began arriving to take them home. Finally, only Tara and Danielle were left to help the Andrewses clean up.

"You must be tired," Mr. Andrews said.

Suddenly it was as if he had reminded her, and yes, she was tired. The only spot of dirt on her uniform was on her right knee, where she had caught herself falling while charging after a bunt. Often her uniform was dirty because of diving after the ball or sliding into a base. But not tonight.

After checking to make sure she would not be getting the chair dirty, Tara flopped into Mr. Andrews's favorite recliner and sighed. The strength to stand seemed to rush from her, and she felt as if she could sit there forever.

Danielle got her Bible and sat on the couch next to her dad's chair. "Just let me read you a psalm," she said.

Tara nodded. In her daily Bible reading, she had come to love the Psalms.

Danielle read, "'Make a joyful shout to the Lord, all you lands! Serve the Lord with gladness; come before His presence with singing. Know that the Lord, He is God; it is He who has made us, and not we ourselves; we are His people and the sheep of His pasture. Enter into His gates with thanksgiving, and into His courts with praise. Be thankful to Him, and bless His name. For the Lord is good; His mercy is everlasting, and His truth endures to all generations.'

"That's Psalm 100," Danielle said.

Tara was on the verge of tears, but she didn't know why. Was it fatigue? She had practiced all week, worked hard in the game, played hard. She had had to concentrate from the first pitch, because her opponents were tough. The Pandas had not scored much either, so one mistake could have cost the game.

Then there was the party, with Suzanne ignoring her. The only thing she could get out of her former friend was a nasty comment.

Tara had run into Suzanne in the hallway, and it was just the two of them. "Suz'," she said quickly, "we can't keep treating each other like this." She didn't know why she had said it that way. The problem wasn't how they were treating each other; it was how Suzanne was treating her. But she didn't want to accuse. She just wanted things back the way they were.

Suzanne said, "Oh, yeah? Just watch me."

Yet here was this beautiful passage from the Bible, telling Tara to be glad in the Lord because it was He who made us. God is good, His truth endures, His mercy is everlasting. What wonderful news! In spite of it all, on top of it all, there is God. He understands. Tara put her face in her hands and let the tears come.

Danielle didn't say anything or do anything. She just let Tara cry. Tara knew Danielle could have no idea why she was crying. Tara thought Danielle would guess that it was because she was tired or upset about her family. In fact, she wasn't sure herself. Part of her tears were from joy. But not all. Her tiredness was not all from the game either. She was tired of the struggle.

Tara had finally realized that nothing would ever be the same again, and no amount of wishing and hoping and working toward it would change that.

"Hey," Danielle said finally. "You remember that game just after you came back from spring break, where you did so well and we lost anyway?"

Tara nodded. "And you told me that was a picture of life."

Danielle smiled. "So I don't need to remind you? You've got it?"

19

"You don't need to remind me, but I'm not sure I've got it. Why does everything have to be so hard?"

"Welcome to life," Danielle said. "It's not fair that you should have to go through this at your age, but we have no choice. We have to deal with what comes our way. You can run and hide, but when you come back, everything will be the same or worse. Suzanne still giving you fits?"

Tara nodded and told her what Suzanne had said.

"You want me to talk to her?"

"No!" Tara said, a little too quickly and much too loudly. "She'd never forgive me for telling on her."

"She's apparently not forgiving you now, but for who knows what?"

"I don't know. It doesn't make sense to me. Is there a word for everything that's going on with me and my family? It seems there should be a word that tells what this is all about. I mean, everybody's messed up. Everything is a mess."

"Chaos," Danielle said quietly.

Tara asked her to repeat it.

Danielle did and explained. "It means messy, messed up, jumbled, out of order, confusion, uproar."

Tara shook her head. "That's perfect. Chaos. That's us."

"What in the world," Danielle asked, "is going on with that woman?"

"My dad's girl friend, you mean?"

"Uh-huh."

"Well, former girl friend anyway. I told you I had talked to her about my becoming a Christian, and it really seemed to bother her. She told me that she and my dad wanted custody of us kids and that no matter what happened, I shouldn't let it affect my faith."

"And she said she had become a Christian when she was about your age?"

Tara nodded. "I found that hard to believe, especially when she didn't seem to care about what she was doing to our family by living with Dad. I told her I would never quit praying for her, and I haven't."

"But she broke up with your dad."

"Yeah. And he blames me."

"He told you that?"

"He told Jeff. And he wants to see me tomorrow."

"We have practice tomorrow afternoon, remember. The tournament starts next Friday, and you're pitching the opener."

"I know. Dad's going to come to practice. I don't think Mom knows."

"Shouldn't you tell her?"

"I don't know. I'm not supposed to really know either. I want to talk to him. I never told him what happened to me."

"Doesn't sound like he's interested."

"He probably isn't, but I'm going to tell him anyway. He's right that his losing Sally, if that's what he wants to call it, is probably my fault. So he might as well know why. I mean, I'm as surprised as he is, and I'd really rather talk to her. She's the only one who can tell me what's going on with her."

"You'd better stay away from her. Talking to your dad tomorrow is going to be tough enough, especially when your mother finds out. You still don't think you should let her know?"

Tara shook her head. "She's been pretty good with me lately. I wouldn't want to give her a reason to keep me from coming to practice. Anyway, like I said, I want to talk to Daddy."

Danielle clapped Tara on the knee. "You OK now?"

Tara nodded. "Guess you'd better take me home."

"Yeah. I got to get going home too. My cat's gonna think I abandoned her."

They both rose, and Danielle thanked her parents for the use of their home for the party.

"Congratulations," her dad said. "And you too, superstar," he added to Tara.

She blushed and thanked him.

"Can't wait to see the Pandas win the city championship," he added.

"We've got a couple of tough games before the finals, Dad," Danielle said. "Didn't you teach me not to put the cart before the horse or count my chickens before they hatch or put all my eggs in one basket or some other cliché like that?"

Her father threw back his head and laughed. "Yeah, I s'pose I did," he said. "But you girls are going to win the city and the state, so your mother and I have cleared our schedule so we can follow you all the way!"

As Danielle drove Tara home, Tara found herself terribly jealous of Danielle's relationship with her father. "That's how it used to be in our home," Tara said. "It really was. I mean, Daddy can say all he wants that the marriage was bad and that Mom was so horrible all the time, but it just isn't true. Our family was close and fun and funny, just like you just were with your dad."

Danielle stopped in front of Tara's house. "We need to keep praying," she said. "I'm not saying anything is ever going to be the way it was. But already it's clear that something is happening in Sally's life, isn't it?"

"Yeah. But what?"

"Maybe you'll find out tomorrow. See you at practice, huh?"

The house was dark as Tara entered and locked the door behind her. She knew her mother would already be in bed because she had to be at work the next morning. And she knew Ray would have been in bed since they got home from the game. Jeff's car was in the driveway, so she thought she might see him before she went to bed. But with the lights off she was surprised to find him in the living room with his girl friend.

They sat there in the dark but not with each other. They were obviously arguing about something, and Tara was embarrassed that she had walked in on them. Both congratulated her on the game, but she left quickly.

She looked in the kitchen and at the bottom of the stairs, then on her bedroom door and in the bathroom upstairs for some note from her mother, some message to say that she had been proud of Tara, that she was glad they had won. Something. Anything. But there was nothing.

3

The Seed

The next day at practice, Danielle was not happy. Tara could tell from the moment she arrived that the coach was distracted and not as quick with a smile as usual.

Suzanne was her own cold self, and some of the girls who didn't get to play often were hanging around her again. Danielle had said that she always worried about the smaller, younger, or less talented girls, because they tended to get bad attitudes after not playing much. When they began running with a starter who also had a problem, a gloomy group could form, threatening team unity.

But that wasn't what Danielle was upset about, Tara soon learned. Tara took it easy in practice, after having pitched a whole game the night before. She did some running, some easy throwing, and some hitting. Suzanne made a snide comment about her acting like a lazy star, and Tara jogged over to her.

Suzanne turned her back and said over her shoulder, "What're you gonna do, beat me up?"

"No! I just wanted to tell you that I'm not lazy and you know it, and that we don't have to talk to each other that way."

Suzanne turned around. "I'll talk to you any way I want to, and I don't care if you're the greatest player in history. OK?"

The last thing Tara wanted to do was burst into tears. She didn't understand this. She certainly didn't need it. She was trying to make things right, and she was crushed. She wanted to cry, to scream, to plead, to beg. But instead she just bit her lip and nodded, then turned back to her business.

After Danielle had finished going over a lot of fundamentals and strategy, she apologized. "I know a team this good and this successful shouldn't need these kinds of reminders, but it never hurts. It's the little things that have put us where we are, and we don't want to forget them."

"Yeah!" Kendra shouted. "Little things like Tara!"

Most of the girls laughed, and Tara was embarrassed, but she worried what Suzanne would think. She sneaked a peek and saw Suzanne looking sour, along with a few others.

Coach Andrews handled it well. "That's right, Kendra. Tara has to be given credit as a superstar player we couldn't have done without this season. But you know what made her the winning player she is?"

"No-hitters and homers!" Wendy said, drawing more laughs.

"Yes, but what allows her to hit and pitch so well?" the coach pressed. "Fundamentals. She works hard, practices hard, thinks, uses her skills. She throws the right pitch at the right time, and when her best stuff isn't working, she adjusts."

Tara was so embarrassed by now that she looked pleadingly at Danielle, hoping that she would change the subject.

Danielle must have got the message. "I have some bad news for all of us," she began. "We've been seeded eighth in the tournament."

She seemed to wait for that to sink in, but no one understood why that was bad news, not even Tara.

"What does that mean?" someone asked.

"Well, they seed the teams in the order of how good they think they are. The tournament officials do it, and where you're seeded determines who you'll play when."

Danielle produced a huge cardboard chart that showed the brackets and pairings. "See?" she said, pointing. "At the top of the first bracket, the first seeded team plays the eighth seeded team. Then the third seed plays the sixth, the fifth plays the fourth, and the seventh plays the second."

"Why?"

"That way they hope that the first two seeded teams don't meet until the championship game. They give them the easiest teams to play first so one doesn't knock the other off early and leave the fans with a boring championship."

One of the younger girls raised her hand. "Why is that bad news?"

"Because they automatically assume that because this is our first year to make it, we're the worst of eight teams. We play the Wildkits, the best team in the city, the defending state and national regional champions, in the first round."

"We're finished," Suzanne grumbled.

"Not necessarily," Danielle said, but to Tara she didn't sound any more convincing than Suzanne.

Something was rattling around in Tara's mind, but Judy beat her to the punch. "That doesn't have to be bad news, does it? I mean, it's insulting and everything, and there's no way I'm gonna be convinced that we're the weakest of the eight league champs in this city, but doesn't that mean that if we can some-how beat the Wildkits and get past them in the first round, we should be able to win the city championship?"

That was what Tara had been thinking, but the reason she hadn't been able to get it out more quickly was that she was re-membering the pre-season tournament at the beautiful, lighted stadium downtown when they had seen the Wildkits play. The team was huge, having lots of players, most of them right at the age limit for that level of girls' softball. They had colorful uniforms and all the equipment. Every girl carried her own leather bag with bats, gloves, shoes, the works.

They had their own cheers and chants, and they were monster pitchers and hitters. In fact, it had been after watching Shelley Kelley, the Wildkits' stocky, stern-faced pitcher, throw a one-hitter in the pre-season championship that Tara realized she herself could pitch that way.

She and Suzanne had raced to Wendy's house and talked her into putting on the catching gear and letting Tara try her stuff. All three girls were amazed at what she had picked up just from watching someone who knew what she was doing.

"That's it!" Tara had squealed. "She lets her legs and back and shoulders do all the work. If I stand like this, apply pressure here, step, turn, and snap my body, the arm motion is natural and the power comes from the body rather than from the arm. It's hard to control, but I can learn that!"

And she had. Hours and hours of practice had hurt her arm before, but with the motion she had learned from watching Shelley Kelley, her arm didn't hurt even after pitching all day. Now she knew why professional men and women fast-pitch pitchers could pitch every game for their teams, sometimes three and four times a day in big tournaments.

Now the girls were arguing about whether it had been good or bad to be seeded last in the city championship tournament, and Tara was snapped back to the present.

"Danielle," she said, "Judy is right. This is a big break. You always tell us not to look past the next game. There's no way we can now. We have to focus everything on that game, and if we get past it, we can think about the next."

"All I meant," Danielle said, quieting down the girls, "was that I was insulted. Insulted for you and me because I know we're better than eighth-seed in that tournament. I know why the organizers did it, and I'm sure the Wildkits have never heard of us and are thrilled to be playing such a weak, unknown team."

"Well, can't they read the papers?" Suzanne asked. "They ought to know we have a great hitting team and at least one undefeated pitcher."

Her point was lost when everybody realized that the undefeated pitcher she was referring to was herself. It was one of the most ridiculous things anybody had ever said about their team. She was implying that because she was undefeated, she was the best pitcher. It was silly. Her average number of runs allowed per game was over eight. Tara's was less than one. Her average number of hits allowed per game was over fourteen. Tara's was less than three. She averaged a walk an inning. Tara averaged two walks per game. Suzanne struck out two batters a game. Tara averaged two strikeouts per inning.

Danielle had the ability to know when to pitch Suzanne. She used her against weak teams with slow pitchers she knew the Pandas could hit well. And they did. They had rocked every opponent of Suzanne's for a dozen or more runs. The two games Tara had lost had come when the Pandas scored zero and one run.

There was no question in anyone's mind—except Suzanne's apparently—that Tara was by far the best pitcher on the Pandas, in the league, in the city, and probably in the state. That's not to say that Shelley Kelley was not a superstar too. She had her share of strikeouts and no-hitters, and her earned run average was under two.

The opening game in the city championship tournament was going to be a pitchers' duel like the fans had never seen.

Suddenly, Suzanne was arguing with everyone. Someone told her she was a jerk and that she was stupid if she thought she was going to throw one pitch against the Wildkits.

"Oh," she said, her voice high and raspy with emotion, "so you don't think the undefeated pitcher is the ace of the squad and should lead the team in the tournament?"

"No!" came back to her in a wave from the team, though Tara had been stunned to silence.

Suzanne was standing now. "Oh, thanks a lot! I suppose I'm to just take this and let big shot Tara Chadwick pitch every inning! Well, why don't we let her hit for everybody too?"

"We'd win easy," Kendra said, breaking the tension. "Hey, Yorty, I thought you and Tara were best friends!"

Suzanne was steaming. "Where've you been, you blind little bat?"

"All right!" Danielle said, standing. "Suzanne, you and I have some talking to do. The rest of you, I'm glad you feel that playing the Wildkits is a good opportunity for us. Practice again tomorrow night at six and every night this week. We play them Friday night at eight."

The girls started to break up when Wendy whispered to Tara. "Your dad's over there."

Mr. Chadwick stood by his car, which he had parked near Danielle's. Tara busied herself with gathering up the equipment.

Suzanne appeared as if she was going to leave rather than talk to the coach, but Danielle hurried to her. "You leave without seeing me, girl, and you can turn in your uniform."

"You'd like that, wouldn't you, coach?" Suzanne snapped. "But I've got news for you. Nobody on the bench wants to replace me either. What would you do then?"

"I'll play eight girls before I'd worry about that," Danielle said. "You want to call it quits?"

Suzanne looked stunned. Tara thought Suzanne had never expected Danielle to call her bluff. Then Suzanne stiffened, and her face seemed to take on a courage Tara hadn't seen before. She knew what her former best friend was going to do. Without thinking, without stopping to consider what she was really doing, Suzanne was going to quit. To show how tough she was and how little she cared about anyone or anybody, that's what she was going to do, Tara just knew. She couldn't let this happen.

She knew Suzanne was bluffing and that she truly loved the game. She couldn't possibly have really believed she was a better pitcher than Tara, but she was hurt, jealous, tired of being number two.

"All right," Suzanne said, "if that's the way you want it, then I—"

"Wait!" Tara broke in. "Don't, Suzanne! Don't! Let's talk first."

"You can just keep out of this, superstar," Suzanne said. "You think you can fix this too? You can do anything, can't you? Pitch, hit, run, and take care of every problem on the team."

"Suzanne, just don't. You may not like me anymore, but I know you, and I know if you quit you'll regret it." She turned to the coach. "Danny," she said, "just ignore whatever she's about to say, OK? Give her a day to cool down, and then see what she wants to do."

Danielle nodded, but Suzanne raged. "No, forget it! I quit."

"Call me tomorrow if you still feel that way," Danielle said. "And Tara, your father is waving at you."

4

Taking the Blame

As Suzanne hurried away, Tara waved to her father so that he would know she was on her way. Then she turned back to Danielle, who was furious. "Danny," she said, "I don't know what's wrong with Suzy, but you can't let her quit."

"Quit? I'm going to kick her off the team if she doesn't quit."

"No, Danny! Something's wrong with her, and until we find out what it is, we have to—"

"Tara! We don't have to put up with this! You've taken more from her the past several weeks than anyone deserves to take. I've seen her attitude, her trying to stir up trouble with the girls who don't play much, her hassling you every chance she gets. Why should we have to put up with that? Her play has gone down, too. She's only the eighth or ninth best hitter on this team, and we can easily replace her in the field."

Tara felt torn. She didn't want her dad to be kept waiting any longer, but she didn't want Danielle to do the wrong thing either. It struck her that maybe Suzanne was right. Maybe Tara did see herself as perfect, the only one who could solve everyone's problems, fix anything. Was that it? Had she become blind to how annoying she could be? Did she come off perfect to everyone?

"Danielle," she said, "I don't know what's the right thing to do, but we both know we can't make decisions when we're mad." She playfully poked her coach in the shoulder. "Especially you, huh?"

Danielle looked madder at first, but then a look of realization came over her. She looked away and sighed. She shrugged. "I guess. But you'd better find out what's wrong with Suzanne and make her get her act together fast, because I'm not taking a team with that kind of a problem into the city tournament."

When Tara left to meet her father, Danielle was picking up equipment and slamming it angrily into the canvas bags. No one had stayed to help, probably out of fear of her temper.

Frederick Chadwick was a different man to Tara this time. She hadn't seen him for weeks, and he was no longer the smooth, glib-talking man with a sparkle of love in his eye. Before he had seemed to enjoy telling Tara about Sally Graves, the young woman who had made him so happy, who had been the answer to his naggy wife, his unhappy marriage. Tara hadn't understood it then, and she didn't understand it now. The only change she had detected in her mother came after she had discovered that her husband was seeing another woman. Then, it seemed to Tara that her mother had plenty of right to be angry.

"OK, here's the problem, Tara," her father began right away when Tara was in the car. "By the way, good to see you. Really good to see you."

Tara nodded and let him continue. It was good to see him too after so long, but she didn't feel like admitting it. She wanted him to cry, to apologize, to tell her he loved her and had seen his mistake. She wanted him to tell her how hard it was to live without his only daughter, to give some hint that it was as hard for him as it was for her. But apparently that was not true.

All he could talk about were his troubles. "Do you know, Tara, that my job is in jeopardy?"

She wracked her brain to remember what that meant.

He explained, "I'm on thin ice. I could be transferred, demoted, even fired if I don't get my performance back up to where it used to be."

Tara had tried the silent approach the first time she had talked to him. She had told him nothing, asked him nothing, challenged nothing. Now she had no fear. "Back up to where it was before you dumped your family, you mean?" she said, her heart racing.

Her father sighed and gave her a disappointed look, as if to say, "You too?"

"No, that's not it at all, Tara. If you want to know the truth, my boss would like to see me working at the level I worked at during the months I was living with Sally."

Tara raised her eyebrows. So it was true. She had left him. Tara had heard and known it must be true, but this was the first she had heard it from her father.

"You know, Tara, I'm pretty high on the totem pole at the corporation."

Whatever that means, Tara thought.

"I was in line for the presidency of the midwest region."

Good for you, she thought.

"But now, unless I get my life in order, I'm going to lose everything."

"You've already lost everything, Daddy, don't you see? You lost everything when you walked out on Mom."

"Yeah, well, maybe, but now she won't have me back."

"You want to come back? Does she know that?"

"Of course she does! But she won't even talk to me!"

"If she won't talk to you, how do you know she knows?"

"I've written to her, called her, pleaded with her . . . "

Tara was confused. She was surprised at her own reaction. This was what she had wanted, what she had dreamed about.

It had been her prayer, and yet now she was not convinced, not happy, not eager to see it happen. She was just curious. What was going on?

"Dad, wait a minute. I heard that Sally had walked out on you and that you were shattered."

"I was! But she won't have me back either, so where am I supposed to turn?"

"So, you're not really sorry about what you did to Mom and us. You just don't have anyone else."

"What I did to Mom! I didn't do anything to your mom! She drove me away, and now I'm willing to forgive her and give her another chance!"

Tara snorted and shook her head. How blind could people be? "That's what you told Mom?"

"Yes! She knows how I feel!"

"And you can't see how disgusting that would be to her?"

Tara's father looked as if she had punched him in the stomach. "No," he said quietly.

"Wouldn't you really rather have Sally back? I mean, the last time I talked to you, she was the greatest thing that had ever happened to you."

"Well, yes, of course."

Of course? What was wrong with this man? How could he not see how he appeared to everyone?

"Then why aren't you pleading with Sally to take you back?"

"Believe me, I have. She won't have me." There was a pause. "It's your fault, you know, Tara."

So there it was—the reason he wanted to see her. She was supposed to do something to fix this. She was the one who could pass a message back to her mother or even to Sally Graves, because she was the one who had talked to each.

"How was it my fault, Daddy?"

"Whatever it was you said to Sally made her run from me. What was it, Tara? What did you tell her?"

"I only told her what had happened to me at Aunt Bev's."

36

"Yeah, I want to know about that. Both your mother and Sally have talked about that. You got religion or something?"

Suddenly Tara was angry. One thing she had wanted to do ever since she had prayed and asked Christ into her life was to tell her father about it. But now, the way he had asked about it, she thought it would be wasted on him. He didn't really want to know anything about God or Jesus or, least of all, her. He just wanted to know what was going on, what had happened to mess up his life.

"I didn't get religion, Daddy. I had all of that I needed from growing up in this family."

He looked shocked. "What is that supposed to mean? We weren't particularly religious. We went to church. I mean, most good people go to church. What's wrong with that?"

Oh, how she wanted to tell him! There are no good people. People who think they're good or who think church will make them look good, those are the ones who go to church without ever really knowing God.

"Church never made a difference in our lives, Dad."

"Well, you can't get carried away with it. Is that what you've done now? Gotten carried away with it?"

It was like talking to a wall. She knew she should try to explain herself, but she sensed her dad was heading somewhere else with this conversation. He didn't really care, didn't really want to know what was going on inside her. He just wanted to find out what she had said to Sally Graves that had made her leave him.

Actually, Tara didn't know. "I became a child of God," she said, trying to sound patient with him.

"Oh, no! That cult? That strange group that believes that, uh, that believes that—"

"Daddy! I don't know what you're talking about! I didn't join any group. In fact, I still go to our church, though I don't get much out of it. I learned that we can be God's children through Jesus because He died for our sins and God forgives us because of that."

She waited to see if her dad was following her at all.

He was not. "Yeah, well, so you told Sally this? You tried to get her to become a child of God or something?"

Tara shook her head. "You tell me," she said. "I haven't talked to Sally except for that one time. I told her what happened to me, and then I prayed for her. That's all."

"Did you upset her?"

"I got the feeling she was upset, but I didn't do it on purpose. I didn't push anything on her." Tara didn't want to speak for Sally. Sally had told her that she had become a Christian when she was about Tara's age. She had drifted away from God and had got into lots of things she was ashamed of. Tara got the feeling that having an affair with a married man was one of those things, but Sally hadn't actually said that. In fact, Sally had encouraged Tara to keep her faith no matter what Sally and her father did. Sally had told Tara that she and her father were planning to be married and eventually that they would want to have Tara and Ray, maybe even Jeff, live with them.

Nothing sounded worse to Tara. She couldn't believe it. She would never allow that to happen, and she couldn't imagine her mother ever agreeing to it either. Sally had hinted that that would be up to the divorce judge.

After Sally had seemed to be so uncomfortable with Tara's story about how she had come to Christ, Tara was shocked to hear her still talking about marrying her father. Apparently Sally had since changed her mind.

"What happened, Daddy? Why did she leave you? What did she say?"

Her father shifted uncomfortably. "Well, something happened to her, she told me. Talking to you had reminded her of who she really belonged to, and it wasn't me. She couldn't justify our relationship, or something like that. She said she was getting back to God, and that she would have to move out. I gotta tell you, Tara, I was hurt. And I don't mind telling you this either: I blame this on you."

5

More Turmoil

"Let me tell you something, Dad," Tara said, sounding very adult, even to herself. "I told you what I said to Sally and that I prayed for her. I was amazed when she told me she had become a Christian when she was a girl, because having an affair with you didn't seem to fit, but—"

"What do you mean? You think God wouldn't like two people finding each other in a world of trouble and disappointment? It may surprise you to know, little girl, that I never felt closer to God than when I was living with Sally. She was so wonderful, so selfless, so giving. I thought I would never meet anyone like her in my life, and when I did, and when we were in love, I know God had to be pleased."

Now Tara was angry. She wanted to leap from the car, slam the door, and run. She wondered what her father would do or say if she did. She wanted to shout at him, to tell him he was stupid, but she knew that would be wrong. It would ruin any chance she would ever have to point him toward God.

She took a deep breath and began slowly, but she knew she still could not hide the frustration and anger in her voice, because from the corner of her eye she could see her father stiffen and look at her curiously. "Daddy," she began, "I have to tell you how ridiculous that sounded, what you just said."

"Ridiculous? I was telling the truth!"

"You may have thought you were telling the truth, and you may be telling the truth about how you felt, but to say that God had to be pleased goes against everything I've ever heard or read about God, even before I knew I could know Him personally. Would the pastor of our church be happy for you because you found this great love, even though it meant leaving your wife and family and living with her?"

Her dad pursed his lips and seemed to be thinking. "All I'm saying is that I wish I had met Sally before I met your mother. We were meant to be, and I believe she would have been God's choice for my life."

Tara was on the verge of yelling again. She wanted to ask him who he thought he was to have any idea what God wanted for him. He had never studied, prayed, or even thought about that, as far as she could tell. He went to church for some mysterious reason, probably because he thought it looked good or was the right social thing to do. But it had never made a difference in his life. She had never assumed that his good points, his sense of humor and the time he used to spend with his family, had anything to do with devotion to God.

What could she say? She was so disappointed, not just in what her dad had done to his wife and her and her brothers but now in his sounding so ignorant. She could hardly make it make sense. This was almost as disappointing as what he had done.

He reminded her of herself when she had been in fourth grade and had made up excuses for why she had cheated on a test and stolen another girl's jewelry. She had been jealous and hadn't studied, but she couldn't admit that.

She had made up some ridiculous story that she told so many times she finally began to believe it herself.

And now here was her father, a grown man, a successful businessman (until now), talking like a school kid. He was going to make what he had done sound like the most logical, right thing to do, even if he had to sound ridiculous doing it.

God's choice for his life? She knew what God wanted for him, but clearly he was not ready to hear it. She changed the subject. "Daddy, what is happening with your job? What is your boss upset about? Did he find out you were having an affair?"

Her father turned and looked sharply at her. "I wish you would quit calling it that!"

"Well, isn't that what it was?"

"No!"

"Well, what do you call it?"

"A romance! We were in love! We planned to be married!"

"Well, OK, whatever. Did your boss find out about it?"

"He knew about it almost from the beginning. He didn't have any problem with it. I mean, he wanted to make sure I was planning to get divorced and marry her. I think he thought things were going to get complicated and maybe messy if I was living with one woman and was married to another."

Tara wanted to cheer. Someone saw that as "complicated and maybe messy" as she did? So she wasn't completely young and naive and stupid?

"But, no, he didn't have a problem with that. His problem came when we broke up."

Broke up? Tara was struck by how much that made her father and Sally sound like junior highers. They were going out, but now they had broken up. "Why was that a problem?" she asked.

"Because Sally was upset. She took more days off, was sick more, and when she was in the office, she cried a lot and sat there looking all red and puffy and upset."

Tara was shocked, but not that Sally had been so upset by the breakup. That was understandable. Maybe she truly had been a Christian and now she felt so guilty that she knew she had to break off with Tara's father, but it was also painful because she had loved him.

What shocked Tara so was the tone of voice her father was now using with her. There was accusation in it. Without saying it right out, he was implying again that he was blaming Tara. Because of what she had said or done to Sally the only time she had been with her, Sally had become a problem employee.

"So that bothered your boss?"

"That bothered everybody! It got back to the big boss, and he wanted to talk to me about it."

"But he hadn't wanted to talk to you about you and Sally before that?"

"Yes, yes, as a matter of fact, he did. He just asked me what my intentions were. I told him we were in love, that I was in the process of getting a divorce, and that we planned to marry as soon as we could. He asked me how my family was taking it. I told him as well as could be expected, and—"

"*I* wasn't taking it well, Daddy!"

"And that was to be expected. You're eleven."

"I'm twelve!"

"Whatever. Anyway—"

Tara was so hurt, so broken that her father did not even know how old she was, that she couldn't decide how to respond. Her anger was surpassed only by her sadness. She was simply brokenhearted. He had been gone long enough to not even keep up with her age.

He continued, "He was happy for us. He wanted to know what I thought about her continuing to work for me after we were married. The company has a policy on that, but he was willing to look into waiving it for me, if that was what I wanted."

Tara was still reeling. Her breath came in short bursts. For a minute she thought she might explode. "What does that mean?" she managed.

"Well, the normal workers are not allowed to work with their husbands or wives in the same department, and especially not work for each other. Here was a situation where my new wife would be working directly for me. I thought we could handle it, and I told him I wanted to at least try it for a while."

"So the big shots get to break the rules, but no one else does?"

Now Tara was accusing, but her father apparently was so impressed that she recognized that he was an important person in the firm that he missed it. He smiled. "Yeah, I guess that's right."

"But even before you could get your divorce and get married, something happened, and Sally became a problem at work?"

"Exactly. Thanks to you."

So he had said it again. It was Tara's fault. Finally, she understood the emotions she had felt when he first accused her. She was not sorry. She had had something to do with the breakup of an affair that had destroyed her family. She was glad, in a way. She hated to see people suffer, but the suffering had been caused by the affair, not by something she had said to Sally Graves.

"So, what happened?" she asked, not reacting to her father's charge. "Did you tell her the boss didn't like her sitting there crying, or what?"

"I didn't have to. Before I could call her in to discuss it, she quit. Every time I tried to make an appointment to see her, she thought I was going to be pleading with her to get her back —which I was—so she would find an excuse to put it off. In her note of resignation, she said she knew her work was below par and that she just couldn't stand to be in the same place with me when she was still in love with me but wanted out of the relationship."

"So she admitted that she still loved you?"

"Oh, yes, and that didn't surprise me. I mean, I'm not saying I'm all that wonderful, but you don't go from loving someone one day to not loving them the next just because of what some young, inexperienced, idealistic kid says to you."

Once again it was a jab at Tara. "You hate me, don't you?"

She wanted so badly for her father to say, "No, of course I don't hate you. I love you, and I hate what I have done to you." But that's not what he said.

"Well," he began slowly, as if not wanting to admit that it was true but unable to say it was not, "I can't say that I'm terribly pleased with you just now. I wish you hadn't talked to Sally, and I wish you hadn't had happen to you whatever it was you say happened."

"Daddy, are you saying you wish I hadn't become a Christian? Is that what you're saying?"

"You've been a Christian all your life, Tara. What do you think we are? We're not Hindus, we're not Muslims, we're not whatever else there is. We're Americans, born and bred, and we go to church. We're Christians."

"Well, Daddy, you couldn't be more wrong, but even if that was true, are you saying that you didn't want me to get closer to God, more serious about Him, learn more about the Bible?"

He shrugged. "I don't know what I'm saying, but yes, that's probably it. You've become a zealous, obnoxious, religious crazy person, and you're causing all kinds of problems."

"*I'm* causing all kinds of problems? Me? You leave your family, have an affair with—"

"Tara!"

"An affair! That's what it was, Daddy! How can you pretend it wasn't?" She didn't stop to let him answer. "You have an affair with another woman, move in with her, plan for a divorce, and even think of trying to get custody of us kids, and—"

"Whoa! Whoa! What a minute! Where did you get that!"

"Get what?"

"That we were planning to try to get custody of you kids. Did your mother tell you that lie?"

Tara knew it wasn't a lie. She also remembered that Sally had told her that she wasn't supposed to talk about it yet. "Mother doesn't know," Tara assured him.

"That's a relief," he said, "but how did you know?"

"How did I know what? You said it wasn't true. If it's a lie, then I don't know anything, do I?"

6

Losing Control

"Tara," her father said slowly, as if talking to an infant, "I have to know where you heard anything about the custody of you kids."

"Why?"

"Because it was very private, very confidential, a big secret—you know what I mean?"

"I'm not stupid, Dad. After all, I'm eleven."

"Yes—hey, I thought you said you were twelve. My mistake. But I have to know—"

"Daddy! Don't you remember when I was born? You always used to tell me you would never forget that night. When was it? When?"

"What are you talking about? I'm trying to get to the bottom of this custody thing, and you're worried about—"

"I'm worried about whether my own father has any idea how old I am!"

"Well, all right! I thought you were eleven, but then I thought you corrected me and said you were twelve. So I misunderstood. I'm sorry."

Tara shook her head. "You're not sorry. And you're wrong again. Now when's my birthday?"

"Uh, it's in the early spring, right?"

"Right! When?"

"Um, wait a minute, don't tell me."

"I'll tell you one thing, Dad. I can tell you when yours is, month, day, and year. Same with Mom, Jeff, Ray, and my four grandparents."

"OK, all right, your birthday is like late February."

"Right! When?"

"The twenty-eighth?"

"The twenty-sixth."

"I was close."

"Now decide what year, and you'll know how old I am."

"OK, uh, let me see. This is summer of—" He was mumbling, but when he subtracted, he brightened. He knew. "You *are* twelve!"

"Right," Tara said glumly. "Would you do me a favor and remember that? For some reason, I don't know why, but it means a lot to me."

"You're a little touchy about this, aren't you, Tara?"

She stifled a chuckle. She was not amused, but she couldn't help laugh at the craziness of this. Her own father had to do his math to figure out how old she was, and *he* thought *she* was a little touchy about it.

"Dad, I gotta get goin' home."

"I know. Just tell me if Sally told you about the custody thing. 'Course, she had to. You don't know any of the lawyers, so if you're not lying about your mother not knowing, then it could have only been Sally."

"Lying. You would accuse *me* of lying?"

"Well, listen, girl, you have gotten me into a lot of trouble lately, and I guess I need to be honest with you and tell you that I don't appreciate it."

Tara grabbed the door handle and slid out of the car.

"Tara!"

Before slamming the door, she yelled at her father. "You are incredible!"

50

She knew she had lost it, but she was out of control now. The rage that had been bottled up was bubbling over.

Her father turned on the ignition so that he could roll his window down and call to her again, but she headed the other way, back to her bike and her glove and bat, which were near the backstop.

Her father wheeled the car around and tried to drive near her, but she stepped off the parking lot and onto the grass. If he wanted to come after her, he was going to have to leave his car. How she wanted that! How she wanted him to realize that it was he who had caused all the trouble! She wanted him to jump from the car and come and embrace her and tell her he was sorry, that he had been wrong. She even wanted him to realize that her coming to Christ was the best thing that had ever happened to her.

But he gave up. He gave up too soon. He parked at the edge of the parking lot and opened the passenger side window and called out to her, but he would not leave the car. "If Sally told you that," he shouted, "I'll kill her!"

Tara should have been afraid for Sally after a comment like that, but she knew her father didn't mean it. She could see that he was still so madly in love with Sally that he had no intention of getting back with her mother. He might be mad at Sally for having told Tara about their plans to get the kids, but what would he do? What could he do? Nothing.

When Tara reached her bike, her father was pulling away. For some reason, that made her even angrier. She grabbed her beautiful aluminum bat, the last gift he had given her before he'd left home months before. It was weighted perfectly and was still white, the way she loved it. Only certain people were allowed to borrow it, and Tara wiped it down after every practice and every game. It still looked new. It was one expensive, perfect bat.

She usually choked up on a bat, setting her hands a half inch to an inch from the end. But now, as she swung at the air with it in her rage, she let her hands slide all the way to the bottom. That usually made the bat feel heavier, but with adrenaline pumping through her body, her mind in turmoil because of her father's accusing her and then driving away, she felt strong enough to swing a bat ten times heavier.

Somehow the effort of swinging was not making her any less furious. In fact, strangely, she felt madder with every swing. Tears stung her eyes, and she tried to pray, but she couldn't. She moved closer to the backstop.

No one was around. Her father's brake lights in the distance were small and faint now. He turned onto the highway. There was no sound except that metal bat whipping through the air. Tara realized she was talking to herself. "What's the matter with me? Am I going crazy? I can't stand this! Who does he think he is, accusing me of causing all the trouble? I was just trying to find out what was going on, just trying to help! I didn't push anything onto Sally Graves! How was I supposed to know she'd been a Christian since she was a child? No wonder she felt terrible when she was reminded of it and knew how wrong she was."

Tara was close enough to reach the silver pole that held the mesh backstop. She stepped and swung at it with all her strength. The loud clang hurt her ears, and her whole body vibrated from the impact. Her hands stung and her arms tingled, and suddenly, something broke loose within her.

She was as angry as she had ever been in her life. It was as if the entire memory of her family's falling apart washed over her and played itself out on a giant screen right before her eyes. She thought of how wonderful her home and family had seemed for so many years, and what a nice guy her big brother was. She thought of the sweetheart of a little brother she had and how cute her friends thought he was.

She remembered her mother and how sharp and smart and pretty she had been. She had a good sense of humor and made a beautiful home. Her father always had time for the family.

But then, with the affair, had come confusion, chaos. Fights between Mom and Dad, Jeff getting into trouble with the wrong crowd, Ray crying all night and becoming sullen. Her mother had become overworked, overtired, neglectful of Tara. And her father! Of all the things he could say or do, what he had just said to her beat all. She had lost her best friend and been accused of causing all the trouble!

She stepped again and bashed her bat against the pole. She saw the ground give way a little and some dust fly. She wasn't surprised to see that she had put a huge dent in her bat, but for some reason, that just added to her frustration. She stepped and swung, stepped and swung, stepped and swung. *Clang! Clang! Clang! Smash!* Her bat was dented and bending. She was crying, swallowing screams.

Why couldn't she quit and pray and get God's help? She loved Him and knew He cared for her, and she hadn't given up on Him. She just needed to let it out. She had told Him. She had told Danielle. But now she felt she needed to do this. She hoped it would make her feel better. So far it hadn't, but still she kept swinging, and clanging, and bashing.

When her bat was broken in two pieces, she looked at her bike and thought about smashing it too. But she was exhausted and humiliated, angry with herself, disappointed at her weakness. She slumped to the ground and sobbed, her mutilated bat reminding her of her family.

As upset as she was, still Tara peeked up occasionally to make sure no one could see her. No one was around, and she could hear no one, but sitting out in the open like that made her feel conspicuous. She looked at her watch. Her mother expected her home in twenty minutes. She tucked her feet up under her, put her head between her knees, and stared at the ground. She sat in the dirt, where it felt cooler than anywhere else. She studied the patterns of cleat marks in the earth, soft from a gentle, morning rain, and felt herself relaxing, her breathing becoming less shallow and her heart slowing. A bead of sweat trickled from under her hair down the back of her neck and made her shiver. The feeling of crying was still in her throat, and when she glanced at her bat, she moaned softly.

Why had she done that? Why had she ruined such a wonderful thing? Why had her father ruined such a wonderful thing? And how could she ever get to him, reach him, convince him, persuade him? It seemed hopeless.

She tried to pray. She didn't know whether to ask forgiveness for what she had done or thank God for allowing her to get it out of her system. Though she felt a little ashamed, the more she thought about it, the better she felt. She had to take it out on something, and she was glad she had not taken it out on a person.

Maybe that was why her mother had been the way she had been. Where else could she release the anger she felt? And what about Suzanne? What was her problem? Could it really all have been because of Tara's new faith? She was acting like an angry, infuriated person, just like Tara had been. Only Tara had beaten her bat against a backstop. Suzanne had used Tara as a target.

The more she thought about that the more convinced she became that there was something else wrong with Suzanne, something she wasn't talking about, wasn't admitting. How could anyone change so quickly? Tara knew she had misjudged Suzanne. She knew Suzanne had never been as loyal a friend as Tara had thought. She knew there had to be a lot of truth to the rumor that behind Tara's back Suzanne said all kinds of bad things.

But that could be explained. There was jealousy, she knew. She could work on that. Suzanne never claimed to be perfect. But this anger, what was causing that? Whatever it was, it was going to run head-on into Danielle's temper, and even though Danielle was a Christian, she wasn't going to put up with Suzanne for long.

That would be bad. Tara agreed that bad attitudes can ruin the best teams, but she wanted to fix this problem with Suzanne before Suz got kicked off the team.

Tara rode to the shopping center where she called home. "Mom, can I be a little late, like a half hour?"

"Why?"

"I want to go talk to Suzanne."

"You'll have to microwave your dinner when you get here. I've got a meeting with my lawyer."

"OK."

"Is Suzanne coming to stay overnight, Tara?"

"I doubt it."

"Well, if she's going to, call me first."

Tara agreed, but as she rode off toward Suzanne's, she shook her head. How could her mother be so blind? Did she really not realize that Tara and Suzanne had not been friends for weeks?

Tara stopped at a dump near the freeway and flung her bat over the landfill and the debris. She watched it twirl like a helicopter blade till it fell, clanging for the last time, among the cans and bricks and junk at the bottom of the ravine.

7

Surprise, Surprise

Tara was scared when she parked her bike at the front of Suzanne's house and approached the door. She didn't know what to expect. Suzanne had been really mad earlier, and she had accused Tara of thinking she knew how to fix everything. What was Tara supposed to say now? That she knew from how she herself reacted to her father that there had to be something else going on in Suzanne's life to make her act the way she did toward Tara?

Tara almost spun on her heel and left. No matter what she said or did, she was going to fall right into Suzanne's trap. Her former best friend had said she acted holier than Suzanne, that she was better than everybody else, that she thought she had all the answers. Plus, she was jealous of Tara for being cuter, having more boys interested in her, being a better hitter, a better pitcher, all that.

Tara couldn't win, and she knew it. Still, she stood there at the door, as if begging to be punished. She reached for the doorbell and almost couldn't move. It was as if her hand was pushing against solid brick and she had been drained of strength. Maybe the Yortys were having dinner. Maybe Suzanne wasn't even home. What if she *was* home but wouldn't see Tara? Why had she decided to do this? Could she leave now, hoping no one had seen her? No! She wasn't a coward.

But what was she? Everything Suzanne said she was? Did she think she was better, knew more? What was she doing here? She reminded herself that she just had a feeling something was really bothering Suzanne, something more than Tara's having become a Christian. How could that bother somebody so much, even if it was a best friend who felt threatened by it? Suzanne had not simply quit being her friend and started ignoring her. Tara might have been able to handle that more easily. Rather, Suzanne had become Tara's enemy, picking on her, making life miserable for her.

Tara finally pushed the button, but even as she heard the bell ring from inside, the door swept open and Suzanne pushed the storm door toward Tara. In that split second before she realized what was going on, she knew that Suzanne had begun opening that inside door before the bell even sounded. And what was she doing with the storm door—trying to push Tara down the steps?

Tara stepped back so the door wouldn't hit her, feeling for the top step with her heel. Suzanne, obviously upset, eyes red and face blotchy, came right out toward her, arms outstretched. Tara flinched as if she thought Suzanne might try to hit her or push her.

But Suzanne didn't slow down. She reached for Tara and pulled her close in a mighty hug, holding her tight and burying her face in Tara's shoulder. Tara didn't know what to say or do.

Suzanne just held her, rocking back and forth and sobbing. Tara slowly brought her hands up to touch Suzanne's back, patting her gently but saying nothing. Tara waited and waited, wondering what to do and whether she should say anything. She prayed silently for the right words or actions, whatever was necessary.

Finally she felt Suzanne loosen her grip slightly, but still she hid her face in Tara's shoulder. Then, without showing her face, as if she was embarrassed to be seen crying, Suzanne turned Tara around and walked her down the stairs, around to the driveway, to the backyard, and around the back of the garage. Finally, she let go, and slid to the ground with her back up against the garage, facing the alley. No one was around.

This had been one of Tara's and Suzanne's favorite spots to sit and talk. No one could see or hear them, and they could share their hopes and dreams and fears and gossip and whatever else they wanted. The place brought back memories for Tara, and she hoped with all her being that this meant some softening in Suzanne. Could it be that they would be friends again?

She sat there, waiting, not knowing whether she should turn and look at Suzanne or just wait. So she waited, staring straight ahead. She heard Suzanne trying to compose herself, sniffing and wiping her face, trying to catch her breath.

"I want to know something," Suzanne managed at last.

"Anything," Tara whispered, trying to signal that she was ready to do whatever she had to do to regain the friendship.

"I want to know how you could have been so good to me when I was so rotten to you."

Now what could Tara say? She believed it was because God was living in her, but saying stuff like that had made Suzanne so mad, why would she want to hear it again?

"I don't think I used to be that way," Tara said. That didn't even make sense. What was she trying to say? Somehow, Suzanne understood anyway.

"I know you didn't. I used to be able to get you so mad you would say nasty things. Then I didn't feel so bad about how I felt and what I did. But not this time. I haven't been able to get you mad for weeks."

"Ha!" Tara snorted. "I've been pretty mad."

"I'm sorry."

Tara thought she would never hear Suzanne say that. "Why?"

"Because I made you mad."

"Yeah, but why are you sorry? You didn't seem sorry then."

"I was."

"You were?"

"You bet."

Tara didn't understand, but she didn't want to ask. Suzanne was going to tell her what was going on in her own good time, and Tara would just have to wait. So she waited. She wanted to tell Suzanne she forgave her, since Suzanne said she had been sorry even when she hadn't appeared sorry. But Tara was afraid she would be sounding as if she thought she was better than Suzanne again, and she didn't want that. It wasn't that she was going to be afraid all the time and try not to say anything that made her sound like a Christian, just because she didn't want to lose Suzanne. Rather, she simply wanted to be more careful than ever. She was supposed to be a good example to people, not an obnoxious one.

"Why did you put in a good word for me to Danielle?"

"I don't know," Tara said. "I just know how much you love the game, and I knew you didn't really want to quit."

"You know me better than anyone, Tara. But I've been so mean to you, I would think you'd want me off the team."

Tara had to think about that. If she was honest, she would have to admit that the team might be better off without Suzanne if she was going to continue to be such a bad influence on everybody, especially the younger girls. "I guess I was hoping," she said, "that if you were allowed to stay on, you might come around, just because you wanted to."

"Well, Danielle called me a little while ago," Suzanne said. "She said she wanted to talk to me. I wanted to put her off, because I could tell from her voice that she was still upset with me. I was still mad too, but I was scared to death I had said too much and that she would take me up on my quitting. You're right. I don't want to quit. And I'm even willing to have a better attitude to stay on the team."

"Did you tell Danielle that?" Tara asked. Because Suzanne had been so upset when Tara got there, Tara thought maybe she had been kicked off the team.

Suzanne nodded. "Not before she told me first. She told me what you had said about me, how you were sure something else was wrong, otherwise I wouldn't be the way I've been. I was so shocked that I couldn't even talk. She was pretty tough with me, Tara. She told me to get my act together, apologize to the other players, straighten things out with the younger girls, or consider myself off the team. But most important, she said that if you hadn't come to my defense, I wouldn't even have this chance. I don't know how to thank you, Tara."

"You're thanking me right now. But I'm still confused."

"I knew you would be. I knew I would have to tell you."

"Tell me what, Suz'?"

"Tell you you were right."

"About there being something else wrong?"

"Uh-huh."

"Do you want to talk about it?"

"Not really, but I owe it to you."

"You don't owe me anything."

"I owe you an apology, Tara."

"You already gave me one. I accept. I forgive you. I mean, that sounds holy and all that, but you were mean to me and you're sorry, so I can forgive you, can't I?"

Suzanne smiled through her tears. "Yeah, you can. Thanks. But I still ought to tell you what's been bothering me."

"I don't mind knowing, Suz', but I want you to know you don't have to tell me if you don't want to."

"I want to."

Tara shrugged. "OK."

"All that stuff I said about you? You know about being holier than me and the perfect person and all that?"

"Yeah."

"I didn't mean it."

"I know. You apologized."

"But I didn't mean it at all. I was mad at you before that, and I didn't know how to tell you. I needed a reason to treat you bad and to get rid of you as a friend, but I didn't have an excuse until you came up with that story about becoming a Christian and all that. I still don't understand that, and I'm not sure I like it, but it's all right. Whatever makes you happy is fine. But I was unhappy. I was miserable. I was going through the worst time of my life, and you didn't even notice."

Tara was stunned. She didn't know what Suzanne could be talking about. "You mean, when I came back from my cousin's and told you all that, I should have noticed that you were upset about something else?"

"No! It was long before that. Tara, you were so wrapped up in your own problems, you didn't even notice mine!"

"Well, what was it? And why didn't you tell me?"

"At first I didn't want to. I was so ashamed, so mad, so embarrassed. I knew I should be able to tell you, because you had been telling me all about your parents for so long, I knew you'd understand."

Tara's heart sank. *Oh, no. Suzanne's parents?*

Suzanne continued. "But we had talked so long about your family and you and your parents and everything, and I had so much advice, I didn't want you to know."

"Know what?"

"About my parents."

"Them too?"

Suzanne nodded, her eyes filling with tears.

"You dad has left?"

"Worse than that. At least it's worse if you ask me. It's my mom. She's having an affair with a guy at work. She wanted my dad to move out, and she wanted to marry the new guy and have him move in. My dad got a lawyer and stopped that from happening, so my mom moved out and she's living with the new guy. Only he's married too, and his wife is hassling them. It's horrible!"

62

Tara felt her own tears returning. She turned and held Suzanne and let her cry. What a lousy, rotten world this could be sometimes. What a lousy, rotten world.

"I'm sorry, Suzanne," she said. "I'm so sorry. Especially that I didn't even know and that I was so wrapped up in my own problems that I couldn't tell."

Suzanne cried and cried. "It wasn't your fault," she said. "But I was sort of hoping when you came with your new religion and everything that maybe you would be even more sensitive."

"Well, I should be! I mean, I am! I just didn't know."

"Yeah. I understand. I guess I was just hoping that maybe you could read my mind or something."

I wish I could, Tara thought. *How I wish I could!*

8

Flowers on the Lawn

I need to ask you something, Suz'," Tara said, "and then I have to go. When people started to notice that we weren't friends anymore, and they saw you being kinda mean to me, well, a lot of 'em said you had never been a true friend. They said that you used to talk about me behind my back."

The girls were sitting apart again, backs against the garage wall, staring into the bushes on the far side of the alley. A small boy rode his bicycle madly past them, swerving to splash through any puddle he could find. A few months before, the friends would have laughed together about that, made some silly comment, kept the joke going all day.

Now they just sat, embarrassed and awkward, Tara having raised the most painful subject of all. Suzanne sat unmoving, then slowly lowered her head until her tears splashed on the ground. "It's true," she said. "I've been horrible to you."

"Why?"

Suzanne shrugged. "I don't know. I was jealous, I guess. I really wanted to believe you were not as nice, not as smart, not as good at sports as you are. I always felt so second best."

Tara didn't know what to say. She didn't want to try to tell Suzanne that she wasn't second best in a lot of these things, but that Tara just didn't care and never thought about it. "Was I irritating about it?" she asked.

"What do you mean?"

"Was I, um, obnoxious?"

"What does that mean?" Suzanne said.

"Did I make you and everybody else sick?"

"Yes!"

"Oh, no! Oh, brother! Did I really? I didn't mean to. Really, I didn't."

Suzanne struggled to her feet and looked at her watch. "You're going to be late. You want me to tell your mom you're on your way?"

"Wait, Suzy. I have to know if I really make people sick."

"Well, of course you do, Tara. But it isn't your fault you're so smart and cute and good at everything. The only way to keep people from being jealous and thinking you're too much would be to play stupid and awkward and ugly."

Suzanne was smiling; Tara wasn't.

"But do I brag? Do I put people down? Do I talk about myself too much? Do I have my nose in the air?"

Suzanne shook her head and put her arm around Tara as they walked toward the front. "No. And that's what bothers everybody so much. You'd be a lot easier to hate if you were stuck up."

"I don't get this," Tara said.

"Believe me, it's a nice problem. Everyone else wishes they had it. Most of us think it would be wonderful to be so good at everything that nobody could stand us."

Suzanne laughed at her own humor, but Tara was still troubled. "What am I supposed to do?" she asked.

"I don't know, Tar'. If I were you, I wouldn't change a thing. I feel real terrible about what a rotten friend I was."

Tara wanted to tell her it was all right and not to worry about it. She wanted to say she forgave Suzanne and wanted to stay her best friend. That was true. But she was so hurt to find out it was true about what Suzanne had done to her, even when she thought they were best friends, that she just had to ask, "What are you going to do about it?"

"About what?"

"About the stuff you said about me."

Suzanne stiffened. "I apologized. What more do you want?"

Tara felt angry. She didn't understand herself. Why was she pushing this? Maybe she had been hurt more than she realized, and she didn't want it to happen again. "I guess I want you to promise to never do it again."

Now Suzanne appeared to be angry. "I said I was sorry. I'm sorry I'm not perfect."

"Suzy! I don't want you to be perfect! I just want a friend who's a best friend, and best friends are loyal to each other."

Suzanne said nothing more. She simply turned and ran up the steps and into her house. Tara wished she still had a bat to smash. Why did everything have to go wrong? Why had she pushed so hard? Why couldn't she have simply accepted the apology and lived with it? She had told Suzanne that she knew about her talking behind her back, so of course Suzanne would quit that.

Tara was mad at herself, mad at Suzanne, mad at her father. She leaped aboard her bike and rode off toward home. She arrived to the strangest sight. It was a picture that would never leave her as long as she lived, one of those horrible moments etched on the brain, never to be erased.

It was humiliating, embarrassing, frightening. Her father was on his hands and knees in the front yard, in his nice business suit. He crawled around, picking up flowers and putting them back into a green piece of waxed paper. Tara's mother stood at the door, screaming at him, not caring what the neighbors thought.

"You come here with a handful of flowers after what you have dragged this family through?" she raged. "You get out of here and never come back! I don't care if I ever see you again!

And if you try to talk to my children again, I'll have you arrested!"

Tara had stopped, fifty feet from the yard. Her mother's screaming could be heard all up and down the block. Some neighbors were out. None looked in the direction of the Chadwick home. All pretended not to hear. But they could hear. Tara knew. They could hear as clearly as she had heard.

Her mother slammed the door, and the storm door slammed shut, too. Her father slowly crawled through the yard, rescuing the flowers his wife had apparently flung over his head.

Tara stood there, straddling her bike, wanting to die. She wanted to dig a hole, crawl deep into it, and cover herself over so no one could see her or talk to her or hear her. She wanted to scream, to sob, to never appear again.

Her father didn't notice her. He moved, as if in slow motion, to his car. He sat behind the wheel for a minute, then started the engine and slowly pulled away. Tara waved, but if he saw her he didn't act like it. There was no wave, no look, nothing. He just slowly drove out of the subdivision.

Suddenly the Chadwick garage door opened, and Tara's mother backed quickly out. The tires squealed as she turned to race off in the other direction. She stopped quickly as she saw Tara.

Her window glided down. "About time you got here!" she said. "Don't you ever talk to him again, you hear?"

Tara nodded. "I hear." She wasn't sure about obeying that rule, but yes, she had heard.

"I've got to see my lawyer," she said. "Jeff is going to take you out for dinner." Without another word, she sped away.

Tara, as if in a trance, walked her bike up into the garage. She felt as if the whole neighborhood was watching her, knowing that she had a family that had been shattered. How could they fight right out there in front of everybody? She tried to pray, but she didn't know what to say. "Help me," was all she could think of. "God, help me."

She was startled when the door from the house to the garage opened and Jeff strode out.

"Let's go, Toots," he said lightly, as if nothing had happened.

"Where's Ray?" Tara asked.

"Mom sent him out the back to Billy's as soon as she saw Dad pull up. Had me call Billy's mom and ask if he could stay there for dinner and until she got home."

Tara nodded. "You heard all that?"

"All that just happened, you mean?" Jeff said, getting in his car and pointing to the passenger door.

Tara got in. "Yeah. You saw that?"

"Course. But, Tara, you gotta pretend it never happened."

"Never happened! Jeff, our parents just had a screaming fight on our front lawn. Our dad was on his hands and knees in his suit, picking up flowers!"

"Tara, Tara," Jeff said quietly as he backed out of the garage. "It never happened. I'm not going to mention it again. You're not. Mom and Dad sure won't. The neighbors will never admit they saw it. They won't ask about it or mention it. It didn't happen. OK?"

Tara felt suddenly older than she wanted to feel. In a way, she sensed Jeff was right, that there might be some truth, even some wisdom, in what he was saying. But another part of her argued against it. Maybe it was good that no one would ever mention such a horrible event again, and maybe it was all right that Tara and the neighbors—both knowing the truth—pretend it hadn't happened.

But it wasn't just the embarrassment, knowing that everybody knew you had parents who hated each other and a family that had come apart at the seams. Tara was horrified at the fact that her parents' future looked hopeless. This was something that might forever put a wall between them. How would they survive this? How could their divorce be slowed, let alone stopped?

This was the worst, the very worst.

"Where do you want to eat?" Jeff asked, and again he sounded so calm she could hardly believe it. He really was going to put this out of his mind.

"I'm not hungry," she said.

"Well, I am," Jeff said. "I'm going through the drive-through. You want anything?"

She shook her head. A few minutes later, as Jeff pulled into the fast food place, Tara said, "You know what I want? I want you to take me to see Sally Graves."

"You're kidding."

"I'm serious."

"I don't even know where she lives." Jeff called out his order and pulled ahead.

"She lives in the tower at the end of the frontage road," Tara said. "At least that's where she lived before she moved in with Dad."

"I'll take you over there, but what do you want to see her for?"

"I just want to know what's going on with her. She dumped Dad, you know."

"I know. Because of you."

Tara felt pain deep in her stomach. As Jeff's order was passed through the window, she knew the pain was as much from hunger as it was from knowing that Jeff too blamed her.

"Sure you're not hungry?" he said. "Have these fries. I'll get more if I'm still hungry."

She took them gratefully, but they were too hot to eat right away. She let the salty potato smell satisfy her while she waited for them to cool.

"Sally did not dump Dad because of me," Tara said.

"Of course she did," Jeff said. "Why else? You hit her with your religious nonsense, remind her of her own childhood church experience, and her conscience goes nuts. Dad didn't have a chance after that. Good work, Tara. You got your wish."

Tara grasped one thin fry and waved it in the air to cool it. "I didn't just wish she'd dump Dad," she said. "I wished he would dump her and come back to Mom."

"Same difference," Jeff said, now parked and his mouth full. "She dumps Dad, and Dad comes runnin' back to Mom. Only thing is, Mom doesn't want him back anymore. Hasn't for months."

"Why not?"

"You don't know that?"

"No."

"Well, for one thing, she knows he's only comin' back on his hands and knees—ha, literally!—because Sally left him. That's the only reason."

Tara slid the fry in the side of her mouth. It was good, tasty. "You think maybe if Dad waits a while, convinces her he's serious and is really sorry, she might take him back?"

"You kiddin'? No way!"

"Why not?"

"Because Mom's got her own thing goin' on the side, that's why."

Suddenly, the fries weren't tasty at all.

9

Chaos II

The child in Tara wanted to pretend she didn't know what Jeff meant. But the girl in Tara who had been through so much during the past several months knew exactly what he meant.

"Mom?" she said, the word sticking in her throat.

"Yeah! Tell you the truth, I'm kind of proud of her."

"Jeff! How can you say that? She's seeing another man?" Tara was less interested in Jeff's disgusting view of it than she was with making sure she understood him.

"Bingo," he said.

"Who?" she asked.

"Her lawyer. I don't know his name."

"Mom's having an affair with her lawyer?"

"I don't know if you could call it an affair yet or not, but they're seeing a lot of each other. Lots of meetings that last a long time."

"Then you're just guessing."

"No, I'm not. It's true."

"How do you know?"

"Dad told me. That's why he's making this big play to get her back. Says he didn't realize what he was giving up until someone else showed interest in her."

"Did she tell him she's interested in the lawyer?"

"No, the lawyer did."

Tara didn't want to hear anymore. She was out of tears, so crying wouldn't help. She handed the rest of the fries to Jeff and sat with her arms folded, watching the sun set.

"You still want to go to Sally's?" Jeff asked.

She nodded, unable to speak. She tried to pray. "Lord," she said silently, "I keep thinking nothing can get worse, but I'm always wrong. When will this end? When will I know we've hit the bottom and things can only get better?"

"What're you gonna ask Sally?" Jeff said.

"I'm not sure. I guess I just want to see if she's serious about what she's done, if she's going to church, coming back to God."

"Now you sound like a preacher, Tara! You gonna be a nun or a missionary or something?"

She wasn't in the mood for teasing. She hadn't tried to sound like anything. Maybe her faith was becoming so natural to her that she was beginning to sound strange to people. She would have to watch that. She wanted Jeff to come to Christ someday, but she had hoped to help, not be in the way. If she sounded too weird, she could be the reason he never became a Christian.

She ignored his question. "I won't be long at Sally's. In fact, if I don't see her car there, I won't even go up."

"I've got to see my girl friend yet tonight," Jeff said.

"No problem."

By the time Jeff drove to the frontage road and to the parking garage at the tower, the sky was nearly black. "Just drive through the garage and see if her car is here," Tara said.

They found the yellow Firebird on the fourth floor. Jeff missed the exit ramp, so he drove to the roof. "I was gonna park on the street and wait for you," he said, "but if there's a spot up here, I'll take it."

There wasn't. Every space in the entire garage was filled. But one car was parked illegally, jutting out from a spot reserved for a compact car. "Guess who's here," Jeff said.

Tara sighed and shook her head. The luxury car sticking out and making it difficult for Jeff to get through was their dad's.

"You still wanna go in?" Jeff said.

Tara shook her head. "Let's wait till he's gone."

"He may be here all night."

"Don't say that, Jeff," Tara said. "They're through with each other."

"Ha! Well, I'll wait till eight-forty-five, but then I'm outta here."

Jeff backed up till his car almost touched the wall. They were in a position where they could see their dad's car, but it was unlikely he would notice them if he came up on the elevator. Tara felt as if this was the saddest duty she had ever done. She was through asking why and how and what, and now she was just numb. If she didn't have God, she knew she had nothing, so she just silently prayed when she wasn't chatting with Jeff.

He turned on the radio to hear the pre-game interviews. She was interested in baseball too, but she tuned out the noise and just sat thinking. Was it still possible she was the cause of all this? Why did she feel so responsible? She had been so close to making things right between her and Suzanne, just because she had felt she should go see her.

Hadn't God been in that? The timing seemed perfect. Suzanne had just heard from Danielle that Tara had put in a good word for her, in spite of everything. Suzanne had realized that she really didn't want to give up softball, and she had had a reason to be so mean lately—her own parents had deep problems.

But it had all gone wrong. Tara had pushed for a promise that Suzanne wouldn't say bad things about her anymore. It had seemed logical at the time, but suddenly she had lost Suzanne again.

Am I going to lose everything and everybody, God? Danielle had told her that sometimes God lets His children get to the point where all they have is Him and nothing and no one else. *I feel like that's where I am right now,* she prayed.

Jeff touched her arm. She looked at him and followed his gaze to the elevator door. Her father came from the elevator, head down, something in his hand. He stuffed it in the trash barrel just before he got to his car. Again he sat there, this time longer than he had in front of the house.

Jeff leaned forward and stared. "I think he's resting his head on the steering wheel."

"I wonder what's going on," Tara said.

"I'd like to know what's in that trash barrel," Jeff said.

"Let's look when he leaves," Tara said, then her blood ran cold. She quickly told Jeff what her dad had said about killing Sally if he found out she had told Tara about the custody battle.

"No way!" her brother said. "Dad wouldn't hurt a flea. He looks pretty down to me. You check the trash bin, and I'll follow him and make sure he's OK."

"Go ahead. You can pick me up later."

Jeff nodded. They waited a few more minutes, which seemed much longer to Tara, and finally they heard their father's car start.

"I'm going to wait until he's on the street," Jeff said, "so I'm not too obvious."

Their father's car was already off the roof and at least a floor below.

"I'm going to go now," Tara said. "I'll look for you in half an hour. Call me if you get hung up."

"Her number's in the book?"

"I think so. If it isn't and I'm not outside waiting for you, just come to her place."

"She won't mind?"

"You know her," Tara said. "Even when she was having the affair she seemed like one of the nicest people on earth."

"What if Dad did do something to her?"

"Then the place will be surrounded by the police when you get back, I guess," she said.

"I gotta get goin'," Jeff said, and Tara left.

Tara looked around before she pushed the swinging door on the trash can. She didn't want to look like a vagrant searching for dinner.

As soon as the light hit the trash, however, she knew what her father had thrown away: the flowers he had tried to give her mother. No wonder he had gathered them up from the yard after she had thrown them. He had tried to use them on Sally as well. Apparently Sally hadn't thrown them, but she hadn't accepted them either.

How sad, Tara thought. *How pathetic.* She knew her father was doing the same thing she was—reaching out to see who was still there for him, desperate to put some order back into his life. He had lost his wife, and now he had lost his girl friend. His wife wouldn't have him back, and now neither would Sally.

Tara stared for a few seconds at the green paper and the broken flowers. Had he really expected Sally to think they were new and fresh? How would she have felt if she had accepted them and considered taking him back, only to learn one day that his wife had first thrown those same flowers onto the lawn?

Tara took the elevator to the ground and walked under a canopy to the lobby. She searched the mailboxes until she found the name "S. Graves." She pushed the button.

There was no response. Was Sally not there? Was that why her father had returned looking so defeated? Maybe that was good news. Tara wasn't excited about waiting in a strange apartment building for a half hour, but it was a nice place and probably safe. She pushed Sally's button again.

She jumped when Sally's husky, emotion-filled voice crackled over the cheap intercom speaker: "Fred, please go away!"

She searched the plate above Sally's mailbox and pushed the intercom button. "Sally, it's me, Tara!"

"Who?"

"Tara. Tara Chadwick."

There was a long pause. Tara knew Sally had heard her this time, and she wondered if Sally would see her.

"I'm not feeling too well right now, Tara. Could you maybe call me or something?"

"I'm sorry," Tara said. "My brother left and isn't coming back for me for a half hour. Is it safe to wait down here? I don't mind. I'm sorry to bother you."

There was another long pause. "I'll buzz the door," Sally called. "Just pull it open when you hear the noise. I'm on the ninth floor, apartment nine two three."

A few minutes later Tara stepped off the elevator and followed a sign to the left. Sally poked her head out from 923 and called out to her. "Down here, hon."

Sally sat in her bathrobe, her eyes red. Tara tried to apologize for bothering her, but Sally refused to hear that. "It's no problem," she said. "It's just that your dad was here, and that was hard for me."

"I know," Tara said, not explaining herself. She certainly didn't want Sally to know that her father had been home before he came here. But she wondered herself why she felt a need to protect him. Maybe Sally should know what he was really like. "Are you all right, Sally?"

Sally nodded. "I'm OK. I'm better than I've been for a long time." Tara couldn't wait to hear why. "It's just that it's hard to give up someone you love, even if that love was wrong. Just because it was wrong doesn't make it go away, and it sure doesn't make it easy to forget."

"You still love my father?"

"Probably always will, though I shouldn't. He's off limits, and he's no better than I am. He was as wrong as I was, giving up his wife and family, cheating, being unfaithful. Only difference is, I knew better."

"He knew better too," Tara said.

"I know, but he's never claimed to be a Christian."

"Oh, yes, he has," Tara said. "He made that very clear to me."

"I know," Sally said. "He said the same thing to me when I first broke up with him. He didn't like me saying that I was a Christian and couldn't continue living with him. He said he was a Christian too, but you and I know the difference, don't we?"

Tara nodded slowly. She wanted to ask what her father had wanted, but she had come to see how Sally was doing. She had been a little envious when Sally had said she was doing better than she had for a long time. Tara wished she could say the same.

"So," she began, "why have you been doing so well, up till a few minutes ago?"

10

Encouragement

Sally Graves moved to a window sill where she plucked several tissues from a box and dabbed at her eyes. "I don't think these are going to do it," she said. "If you don't mind, I'm going to wash my face."

When Tara was alone in the living room she could see why Sally had enjoyed the "better" life with her father. Tara knew Sally made good money for a secretary, but probably one tenth of what her father made. Sally's place was nice, and she enjoyed many comforts, but it was a long way from the beautiful condo Tara's father had rented for them.

Still, there was something homey about this little place. There were pictures of family and friends, handmade knick-knacks here and there, and low, warm lighting.

Sally emerged, drying her face. "I should not have let your father come up here," she said. "He said he just wanted to give me something. I told him he could come only to my door, which was a mistake because even that looked bad. Just as I feared, he really wanted to come in. And all he had brought me were a handful of flowers. I refused them and talked to him for a few minutes. It was very painful. I'm afraid I hurt him."

"How?"

"I told him he should go home and give those flowers to his wife. Well, he didn't need a lecture or a sermon from me. He has to do what he has to do."

Tara was confused. "Sally, I may be impolite or pushy or something, and if this is none of my business, you can just tell me."

"Oh, believe me, Tara," Sally said, "anything that has to do with your father and me is your business. It always has been, but never more than since you talked with me the first time. It was why I broke off our affair, you know."

"I heard. But I want to hear it all."

Sally shook her head. "It's just that you were right. I knew good and well that your father did not have a bad marriage. He didn't complain about your mother until we were interested in each other. In fact, before that I thought he was devoted to her. I envied their marriage. I even told him that. I think he thought I envied her because she belonged to him. I should have made that more clear, because all that did was speed up our relationship."

"So you broke up with him because you remembered that he really didn't have that bad a marriage?"

"Well, that was a big part of it, but you know the real reason."

"I think I do."

"You do. You reminded me that I was a Christian. It isn't that I had forgotten. It's just that I had spent so many years drifting from God that I was able to justify everything I was doing or not doing. I hadn't been to church for years, hadn't read my Bible, and prayed only when I was in deep trouble, but I was in deeper trouble than I knew."

"But after our talk you said that I shouldn't let anything shake my faith, even if you and my father got married and wanted custody of us kids."

Sally nodded sadly. "You see how messed up I was? Even though God really spoke to me through you, convicted me, showed me how guilty and wrong I was, still I was trying to leave windows open to do what I wanted to do. Somehow, when I got away from you, I was going to talk myself back into living for myself. I'm glad God wouldn't leave me alone, and I'm glad you had the courage to say what you said, especially to pray for me. That's why I've been coming to your games. I kept hoping your parents wouldn't be there and that I would get a chance to thank you personally. Your being here tonight is an answer to prayer."

"God wouldn't leave you alone?"

"I'm telling you, Tara, He worked on me big time. I felt deep in my heart that I had been wrong, that there was no more hiding it or pretending it wasn't so. I could tell myself over and over that I deserved to do what I wanted, but I could not make myself believe it anymore. I even decided to break up with your father in a month, but in my spirit I felt God absolutely refusing. It was as if He was saying directly to me, 'The only answer is to stop now, tell him immediately, and be done with it.'"

"And so you did?"

Sally nodded. "I drove straight to the apartment, packed everything, left him a note, and moved back here. I told him as much as I could in the note and begged him not to call me before I called him. From that night on I got a completely different view of your father than I had ever had."

"Like how?"

"First, he didn't honor my request. He called almost immediately. I told him I wasn't ready to talk yet, and he got mad and started yelling. I hung up on him, and he kept calling back, ringing and ringing and ringing the phone until I had to leave it off the hook.

"Then he came over here, and I wouldn't buzz him through. He called me on the intercom and cried right there in the lobby."

"He cried?" Tara repeated, suddenly feeling for her father.

"He cried and made a scene. He even pleaded with one of the other tenants to let him come in with them so he could just talk to me. Luckily, they called me first to see if it was OK. I told them no and then called the manager. The manager came and had to threaten to call the police before your father left."

"That's awful!"

"It gets worse. He started sending me letters, telegrams, flowers, candy, expensive gifts like jewelry, even a fur coat."

Tara sat shaking her head. "What did you think?"

"I wondered what I had ever seen in him. How could he be so weak, so dependent? His actions had the opposite effect of what he wanted. I sent all that stuff back to him, refused it as soon as I saw it was from him."

"Did you ever see him again?"

"Sure. I saw him at work before I realized I was going to have to either quit or get transferred to another department."

"Because it was too hard to be around someone you loved but didn't want to see?"

"He was making life miserable for me. He kept asking to see me in his office, and I kept telling him that I didn't want to have any personal meetings on work time. He reminded me that we had had many in the past, and I reminded him that that was over. I told him that when I felt I was able to see him, I would talk to him one last time."

"And did you?"

"I tried to. I thought it was the last time. He hasn't given up. Tonight was proof of that."

"Tell me about that last time, the meeting you thought was going to be the last."

"Well, it came after I felt I had gotten myself squared away in church. My old church is only about thirty miles south of here, on the Wisconsin-Illinois border. I went back there and confessed to my pastor and to one of the women in the church. They prayed with me and believed I was truly sorry and repentant, and I told them I had broken off the relationship. They agreed I should have one final meeting with your father, but that it should be in a public place where he wouldn't cause a scene, and that a friend should be prepared to drive me home so he couldn't pressure me into going anywhere with him."

"So, where did you have the meeting?"

"Well, a lot of things happened first, Tara. I had to confess to the congregation of my church."

"Oh, no."

"It was the hardest thing I have ever done, but you know something? I was glad to do it, to quit living a lie, to get it off my chest. There were some who knew me when I was younger who seemed upset with me and wouldn't speak to me afterward, but most of them, even the new people, were very warm. I'm under discipline and restoration now."

"What does that mean?"

"Well, I had never withdrawn my membership from that church, so they asked me if I would submit to their authority. Believe me, I was glad to. I felt safe and protected, and I knew they loved me and wanted to help me. I am being discipled by an older woman there. She studies the Bible with me and prays with me once a week. She also checks up on me, makes sure I'm still doing what I should and not doing what I shouldn't.

"I am expected to be in church and Sunday school every Sunday, and I can't be involved in any form of leadership or public ministry for at least a year. Then my counselor can make a recommendation. In a year, they might let me sing in the choir, but it will be longer before I could teach Sunday school or work in one of the youth programs."

"That sounds pretty hard," Tara said. "Why so strict?"

"Oh, I don't blame them. I put myself in their shoes, and I don't think I would want people teaching my kids or being active in a public ministry very soon after they had been living in sin the way I was."

"Aren't you humiliated to have everyone know?"

"Of course I am. It's horrible. But it's also a price you pay when you do what I did."

"It's only a price you pay if you want to admit it."

Sally smiled. "Yes. But the price for hiding it is even higher. There's never any peace. Who wants that?"

"So how did it go with Dad?"

"Well, we met at a restaurant downtown. My aunt agreed to pick me up in an hour and a half. Your father showed up in a new suit, wearing a flower in his lapel. He had a corsage for me, for which I thanked him but politely refused to wear. We didn't talk much before the meal but busied ourselves in small talk about the menu and all that. I was not particularly dressed up, but he kept complimenting me on how gorgeous I looked. He pouted for a while about my not wearing the corsage, and I told him I thought it was inappropriate under the circumstances. He told me that flowers for someone like me were never inappropriate, but he wasn't convincing me. Finally, I had to be very direct with him."

"How?"

"I wasn't very hungry, so when I was finished with my meal, I looked him in the eye and said, 'Fred, I have to talk to you, and I want you to listen. This meeting was my idea, not yours, and it is for the purpose of my telling you why I will not be seeing you again. It is not for the purpose of your making a good impression, trying to win me back, or trying to change my mind. Understood?'

"He said, 'You can't blame a guy for trying, can you?' I told him, 'Yes, I can, because you keep trying to convince me that you still have feelings for me and that you want what is best for me. I'm asking you to back off, and you're not backing off.' 'OK,' he said, 'I'm sorry. I'll try.'

"I told him I wanted him to do more than try. And then I told him the whole story, completing what I had begun to him in the original note. I told him about my faith, my church, my confession, my discipline, and my restoration process."

"What did he think of that?"

"I'm not sure. He looked sick. He said, 'Well, I don't suppose I can compete with God.'"

11

Starting Over

By the time Tara had heard Sally's whole story, she was exhausted. "I sure wish I could visit your church sometime," Tara said, "but something tells me my mother may have something to say about that."

"I suppose," Sally agreed. "It wouldn't look too good for me to be hanging around with the daughter of the married man I had been living with. But someday I hope you do get into a good church that really teaches the Bible and where people care about keeping each other accountable before God."

Sally started when the intercom buzzed. "Who is it?" she asked.

"Uh, Jeff Chadwick, ma'am. I'm here to pick up my sister."

"She'll be right down."

"Ask him how Dad was."

"I'd better not. You can ask him when you get down there."

Tara told Sally how they had noticed their fathers's car and Jeff followed him to be sure he was OK.

"Jeff sounded calm," Sally said. "I'm sure if there was anything wrong, he would have said something."

Tara told her about her father's threat—if Sally had told her about the custody idea.

"Oh, he asked me, and I admitted that I had told you," Sally said. "It's all in the past now. There's only one thing I regret."

"What's that?"

"I should have probably accepted the flowers. I just couldn't because I didn't want to give him the wrong signal. If they hadn't looked so ratty, I wouldn't have wanted them."

"You noticed that they looked pretty bad?"

"They looked horrible. They looked as if he had had them in his car for a couple of days. That was why I wanted them."

"I don't get it."

"You see, Tara," Sally said, walking her to the elevator, "those flowers reminded me of something. They were supposed to be beautiful, but they looked horrible. Who knew why? Something had happened to them, and they turned out the opposite of how they were supposed to. I would have liked to put them in water and see what God could do to them. If He restored them, they would remind me of me."

Tara pushed the button for the elevator. "I wish you would have taken them too, but I see why you couldn't."

Sally nodded. "I'll be praying for you and your family, Tara. I think your dad will want to come back eventually, if your mother will have him."

Tara was tempted to tell her what she knew about her mother and her lawyer, but she didn't want to get into that. When the elevator arrived, Sally gave her a tight hug, and Tara nearly cried. "I'll pray for you too, Sally," she said, as the door closed.

She was still fighting tears when she saw Jeff in the lobby.

"What's wrong with you?" he said. "Dad was fine. He just went back to the office. I suppose his condo is a little empty and lonely. At least I hope it is."

Jeff laughed at his own joke, but Tara didn't find it funny. She realized that she couldn't tell Jeff much of what Sally had said, because he wouldn't understand.

When they got on the elevator in the parking garage, Tara pushed level five, but Jeff told her, "I found a spot on two." He pushed that button.

"I'll meet you there," Tara said. I have to get something."

When she arrived at the car a few minutes later she was cradling a wrinkled piece of green paper that surrounded a mess of broken, already-wilted flowers.

"What do you want with those?" Jeff asked.

"I just want to plant them, see if they can still grow."

"Mom's not gonna want to have those things anywhere near our house."

"That's true," Tara said. "Drop me at Suzanne's for a minute, will ya?"

"How long do I hafta wait?"

"Not long, I hope."

Once again, Suzanne was glad Tara had come.

"I'm sorry," Suzanne said. "I just didn't know how to deal with my anger. I shouldn't have walked away from you."

"That's all right. I deserved it. I should have just accepted your apology at face value, and I do."

"Then we can be friends again?" Suzanne said.

"Of course. And I have brought these to prove it."

Suzanne laughed. "This is a joke, right? Tara, I don't want to start our new friendship out wrong, but I have to be honest with you. These look terrible!"

That made Tara laugh, and the more she laughed, the closer she came to crying, and soon she was. The flowers *were* ugly. They represented all that had gone wrong in her life for almost a year. Even though she had become a Christian and had a loyal and true Friend who would never leave her, there were no promises that all her troubles would vanish. In fact, she had more than ever, and they all seemed to be getting worse.

But Sally had been right. The flowers could represent hope and promise and the way things should and could be. "Let's look at these as our friendship," she suggested. "And let's re-plant them to see what happens to them."

Suzanne loved the idea, and by the light from the lamp near the garage they dug around in the dirt in the alley. They didn't know that cut flowers don't grow roots. Planting them just seemed a fun thing to do.

Jeff honked for Tara, and she came running. "I have to see my girl friend tonight yet," he reminded her. "I think she's gonna give me the bad news."

"She's breaking up with you?"

He nodded. "Think so."

"Can you handle it?"

He shrugged. "There are a lot more where she came from."

So that was how Jeff was dealing with everything. He thought it would be easy. He was sassy. No big deal. Roll with it. She wondered how it would be for him some day when it all came crashing down around him.

When they got home their mother was there. When Jeff left to see his girl friend, Tara was alone in the living room with her mother. Ray was in bed.

"How was your dinner?" her mother said.

"I wasn't hungry," Tara said. "But I am now. Can I have anything?"

Her mother chuckled. "I would like to fix you something. What would you like?"

Tara was startled. What had got into her mother? She sounded like she had months ago, before she knew anything about Tara's father's affair. Tara wondered if she were in love too and if that gave her extra bounce in her step, more liveliness in her personality.

"You know what I really have a taste for?" Tara said.

Her mother's eyes danced. "I'll bet I do, because I have taste for it, too. You'd like extra chewy brownies with chocolate frosting and whipped cream."

"How did you know? You're exactly right!"

"Let's make some."

Tara couldn't believe she was going to work in the kitchen with her mother, something she hadn't done in months. Part of her didn't want to have anything to do with her mother because of what she had heard from Jeff, but she was so desperate to have back the woman she once knew that for now she chose to put that out of her mind.

Mrs. Chadwick was just short of bubbly as they mixed the ingredients and pre-heated the oven. "You know," she said, "we haven't done this in a long time. Too long."

"I know, Mom."

"It's like you've grown up right before my eyes and I missed it. I mean, I see you on the ball field, and I'm proud of you and all that, but I've been so busy with this divorce and everything that I . . ."

"Mom, are you going to go through with it?"

"The divorce? Yes. Your father has become even worse. Overbearing."

"He wants to come back."

"He doesn't know what he wants. He's hardly attractive these days, begging, sniveling . . ."

"I still feel a little sorry for him."

"You would. You're that way. I guess I do too, a little. But I will not have him back. Getting rid of him is going to be a little more complicated than I thought, though. I fired my lawyer tonight."

"You did? Why?" Tara was desperately afraid her mother was going to say that because she had fallen in love with him, it would not be appropriate for him to represent her in a divorce case.

"He got fresh with me."

"You're kidding!"

"I'm not!" Her mother was smiling.

"Mother, that's awful! How can you act so happy about it?"

"I was flattered! I haven't had a man show interest in me for so long I can't even remember!"

"But you're not interested in him?"

"Interested in him! Tara! I'm a married woman! And even if I wasn't, I'm not that kind of a woman!"

"You sure seem chipper for just having fired your lawyer."

"Well, I had a major fight with your father, which you saw, and which I'm sorry you had to endure. I was ready to push the divorce as fast as I could. I still am. But when I went to see my lawyer, he started in with this line about what perfect timing it has been that we 'found each other' right when I had a need for a man in my life. I could have bopped him one. I almost did. It was all I could do to keep a straight face when I told him off, fired him, and left.

"As soon as I got home there was a message waiting for me. I called him back, and he pleaded with me not to turn him in to the review board. He said it was just a misunderstanding. He thought I felt the same about him as he felt about me. I had to laugh. That made him feel better.

"But then he told me that he had already told your father that he thought he and I might be interested in each other. I promised him I wouldn't report him—though I should—and then I told him that for saying that to your father alone I would never consider rehiring him. So tomorrow I have to find a new lawyer."

"I still can't get over how up you seem."

Tara's mother sat in a kitchen chair. "I'm not really," she said. "But there aren't many things to laugh about in my life these days. I have to take what I can get. I lost my husband, my husband lost me, Jeff is losing his girl friend . . . "

"I almost lost my best friend."

"Suzanne? You did?"

"Yeah, but we're back together. We're gonna work it out."

"Good for you. You heard about her parents?"

Tara nodded.

"Life's a mess, Tara girl. A real mess."

True, Tara thought. *But Sally was proof that God can turn a mess into something beautiful.*

And Tara's longing was to be another example of what God could do. For now she was going to pray that this "misunderstanding" her mother had with her lawyer would slow down the divorce process enough that something good might come from it.